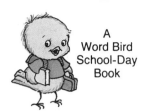

A
Word Bird
School-Day
Book

WORD BIRD'S MAGIC WAND

by Jane Belk Moncure

illustrated by Linda Hohag

color by Lori Jacobson

Created by

THE CHILD'S WORLD

D1279434

Library of Congress Cataloging in Publication Data

Moncure, Jane Belk.
  Word Bird's magic wand.

  (A Word bird school-day book)
  Summary: Word Bird and his friends use their magic
wands to make signs, stories, and a variety of words.
  [1. Vocabulary—Fiction.   2. Pencils—Fiction]
I. Hohag, Linda, ill.   II. Title.   III. Series.
PZ7.M739Wog   1990   [e]   90-1645
ISBN 0-89565-580-2

WORD BIRD'S MAGIC WAND

"Today is my mama's birthday,"
said Word Bird. "I will paint a
picture for her."

4

When the paint was dry, Word Bird wrote some words with his pencil. "My pencil is a magic wand. Look what it can do," he said.

"My pencil is a magic wand
too," said Bee. "I can write
words with it, just like you can.
My card is for my friend. She is
sick."

"I like your pictures and your
words," said Miss Beary.

"I want to write words," said
Frog.

"Me too," said Duck.

"Here. Have a magic wand,"
said Word Bird.

"We can make picture words
with our magic wands," said
Miss Beary. "Let's fill this box
with toy words."

Frog made a robot. Duck made
a truck.

What did Word Bird make?

The next day, Word Bird and
Frog made number words.

Miss Beary made word banks
for them. "You can put your
number words in your word
banks," she said.

Every day Word Bird wrote
words with his magic wand.
He wrote words on signs he
made for his zoo.

He helped make signs for Cat's airport.

"Thanks, Word Bird," said Cat.

Others made signs too. Pig
made a lunch sign with her
magic wand.
"Yum, yum," said Word Bird.

Dog made a news sign with his magic wand. Cat did not like the news. But Duck did.

One rainy, spring day, Miss
Beary said, "Tell me about
funny things you like to do."
Then she made signs with
her magic wand.

Word Bird and Duck helped
her put the signs all around
the room.

"Read my signs, and do what
they say," said Miss Beary.

Word Bird giggled. "What a wacky walk," he said.

Another day, Word Bird wrote a
secret note with his magic
wand. Guess where he hid it?
He put the note in his lunch box.

He gave it to Duck to read at
lunchtime. Was Duck surprised!

All year Word Bird wrote with a
magic wand. One day he cut
out a big, paper circle. He
wrote words around and
around it.

Then he gave it to Duck.
"Turn it around and around,"
he said. "You can read it. It's
my circle story."

Then Word Bird wrote his very own book. Guess what it was about?

He read his book to the class,
and everyone clapped.
"I can write a book too," said
Mouse.

Mouse held up his book.
"Guess who lives in my house?"
he said.
"Who?" asked Word Bird.
"Read my book and find out,"
said Mouse. So Word Bird read
about Mouse and his Mama,
Papa, and Grandma.

Bee made her very own ABC
book. `` `A' is for apple. `B' is for
you, Word Bird,'' she said.
``Wow!'' said Word Bird. ``That's
neat.''

"I have a surprise for you," said
Miss Beary. She gave buttons to
Word Bird and his friends.
"What do the buttons say?" she
asked.

"I am an author," said Word Bird.

You can be an author too. You can write a book with your magic wand.

You can read and write these words with Word Bird.

toy words   dinosaur   robot

food words   pizza   cookies

number words   two   three

signs   zoo   airport

circle story   The most exciting day of my life was the day I went to the zoo.   zoo

shape book   My Dinosaur Book by Word Bird